For LC and FTB
—A. H.

To Kathleen Cooke for her great
dedication to reading
—S. B.

ALADDIN

An imprint of Simon & Schuster Children's Publishing Division

1230 Avenue of the Americas, New York, NY 10020

First Aladdin paperback edition August 2009

Text copyright © 2009 by Simon & Schuster, Inc.

Illustrations copyright © 2009 by Steve Björkman

ALADDIN is a trademark of Simon & Schuster, Inc., and related logo is

a registered trademark of Simon & Schuster, Inc.

READY-TO-READ is a registered trademark of Simon & Schuster, Inc.

For information about special discounts for bulk purchases, please contact

Simon & Schuster Special Sales at 1-866-506-1949 or business@simonandschuster.com.

The Simon & Schuster Speakers Bureau can bring authors to your live event.

For more information or to book an event contact the Simon & Schuster Speakers

Bureau at 1-866-248-3049 or visit our website at www.simonspeakers.com.

Designed by Christopher Grassi

The text of this book was set in Century Schoolbook BT.

The illustrations for this book were rendered in ink and watercolor.

Manufactured in the United States of America

2 4 6 8 10 9 7 5 3 1

Library of Congress Cataloging-in-Publication Data

Heller, Alyson.

After-School Sports Club : soccer day / by Alyson Heller ; illustrated by Steve Björkman.

— 1st Aladdin Paperbacks ed / p. cm. — (Ready-to-read)

Summary: At the After-School Sports Club, Sammy is not as good at soccer as the other children,

but he keeps trying to improve before the parents come for Open House.

ISBN 978-1-4169-9410-7 (pbk. edition : alk. paper)

[1. Soccer—Fiction. 2. Schools—Fiction. 3. Determination (Personality trait)—Fiction.]

I. Björkman, Steve, ill. II. Title. / PZ7.H374197Af 2009 / [E]—dc22 / 2009019974

AFTER-SCHOOL SPORTS CLUB
Soccer Day

Written by ALYSON HELLER
Illustrated by STEVE BJÖRKMAN

Ready-to-Read

ALADDIN
New York London Toronto Sydney

It was the first day of the
After-School Sports Club.
Caleb, Sammy, Alyssa, Tess,
and J.B. were excited to
learn a new sport.

"There are all kinds of
sports we can learn,"
said their teacher, Mr. Mac.

"There's tennis, T-ball,
and soccer."

"Let's try soccer," said Tess.
"That looks like fun!"

Mr. Mac gave each of them
a soccer ball. The kids were
kicking balls everywhere!

Tess, J.B., Caleb, and Alyssa
were doing well. They even
kicked the ball into the
net a few times!

But Sammy wasn't doing so well. He was kicking the ball to the side, and above and around the net.

At the end of the day,
Mr. Mac gathered up
the group.

"In a few weeks, we are going to have an open house so your parents can see what you have learned," Mr. Mac said.

Alyssa, Tess, Caleb, and J.B.
were excited. But Sammy
was worried.

His dad used to play
soccer, and Sammy didn't
want to disappoint him.

When Sammy went home
that night, he told his dad
about the club.

"That sounds like a lot of
fun," said Sammy's dad.
"I can't wait to come see you
at the open house!"

The next few weeks, Sammy
kept on practicing.

But he couldn't kick the ball very far.

He still couldn't
make the net.

And his passes missed!

The night before the big open house, Sammy told his dad that he wasn't as good as the other kids.

"Don't worry," said Sammy's dad. "Just keep trying and do your best!"

The next day, all the kids'
parents came to the
open house.

The kids all lined up and dribbled the ball the whole length of the soccer field.

Next they showed off
their passing moves.

Finally, each kid took a
turn kicking the ball at
the goal.

Tess and Caleb kicked
theirs right into the net.
So did Alyssa and J.B.

Soon it was Sammy's turn.
He took a deep breath.

And kicked the ball—right
into the goal!

"I knew you could do it,"
said Sammy's dad.
"I'm very proud of you."